Goldilocks and the Three Puppies

Goldilocks and the Three Naked Mole Rats

Goldilocks and the Three Elephants

...ocks and the ...e Cavemen

Goldilocks and the Three Whales

Goldilocks and the Three Giraffes

Gold... Th...

Goldilocks and the Three Mosquitoes

Goldilocks and the Three Lions

Goldilocks and the Three Moles

...d the ...es

Goldilocks and the Three Terrible Monsters

Goldilocks and the Three Apes

Goldilocks a... Three Prin...

...ocks and the ...ee Geese

Goldilocks and the Three Giants

Goldilocks and the Three Chickens

Gol... T...

...d the ...ees

Goldilocks and the Three Penguins

Goldilocks and the Three Cyclopes

Goldilocks a... Three M...

...ocks and the ...ee Bunnies

Goldilocks and the Three Dogs

Goldilocks and the Three Germans

Gol... T...

...the ...as

Goldilocks and the Three Goldfish

Goldilocks and the Three Pumas

Goldilocks a... Three Tig...

...ocks and the ...e Nutrias

Goldilocks and the Three Rocket Scientists

Goldilocks and the Three Ants

Gold... Th...

...the ...oi

Goldilocks and the Three Meerkats

Goldilocks and the Three Goats

Goldilocks a... Three Cov...

...ocks and the ...e Big Feet

Goldilocks and the Three Baboons

Goldilocks and the Three Wild Boars

Gol...

GOLDILOCKS

and the

THREE DINOSAURS

As Retold by

MO WILLEMS

BALZER + BRAY   *An Imprint of HarperCollinsPublishers*

ONCE UPON A TIME, there were three Dinosaurs:
Papa Dinosaur, Mama Dinosaur, and some other Dinosaur
who happened to be visiting from Norway.

One day for no particular reason, the three Dinosaurs
made up their beds, positioned their chairs just so,
and cooked three bowls of delicious chocolate
pudding at varying temperatures.

"OH BOY!" said Papa Dinosaur in his loud, booming voice.
"IT IS FINALLY TIME TO LEAVE AND GO TO
THE . . . uhhh . . . SOMEPLACE ELSE!"

"YES!" continued Mama Dinosaur. "I SURE HOPE NO INNOCENT LITTLE SUCCULENT CHILD HAPPENS BY OUR UNLOCKED HOME WHILE WE ARE . . . uhhh . . . SOMEPLACE ELSE!"

Then the other Dinosaur made a loud noise that
sounded like a big, evil laugh but was probably
just a polite Norwegian expression.

The three Dinosaurs went Someplace Else and were definitely *not* hiding in the woods waiting for an unsuspecting kid to come by.

Sure enough, five minutes later a poorly supervised little girl named Goldilocks came traipsing along.

Just then the forest boomed with what could have been a Dinosaur yelling "GOTCHA!" but I'm pretty sure was just the wind.

The loud noise was immediately followed by *another* loud noise that sounded kind of like "BE PATIENT, PAPA DINOSAUR! THE TRAP IS NOT YET SPRUNG!"

But that could have been a rock falling. Or a squirrel.

GETTING CLOSER!

Either way, Goldilocks was not the type of little
girl who listened to anyone or anything.

For example, Goldilocks never listened to warnings about
the dangers of barging into strange, enormous houses.

So as soon as Goldilocks came
across a strange, enormous house,
she barged right in.

Inside, Goldilocks immediately smelled the three bowls of delicious chocolate pudding.

"Mmmmm!" said Goldilocks. "That chocolate pudding smells delicious. If only I could get all the way up to the top of that counter!"

Then Goldilocks noticed a very tall ladder that just happened to be there and certainly wasn't left on purpose.

Goldilocks climbed up the ladder
and found herself face-to-face
with three gigantic bowls
of chocolate pudding.

The first bowl of chocolate pudding was too hot,
but Goldilocks ate it all anyway because,
hey, it's chocolate pudding, right?

The second bowl of chocolate pudding was too cold,
but who cares about temperature when you've got
a big bowl of chocolate pudding?

Not her.

The third bowl of chocolate pudding was *just right*, but Goldilocks was on such a roll by now, she hardly noticed.

Soon Goldilocks was stuffed like one of those delicious chocolate-filled-little-girl-bonbons (which, by the way, are totally *not* the favorite things in the whole world for hungry Dinosaurs).

Tired and groggy, Goldilocks noticed three chairs in the living room. So, she climbed down the ladder and walked out of the kitchen.

The first chair was too tall.

The second chair was too tall.

But the *third* chair—

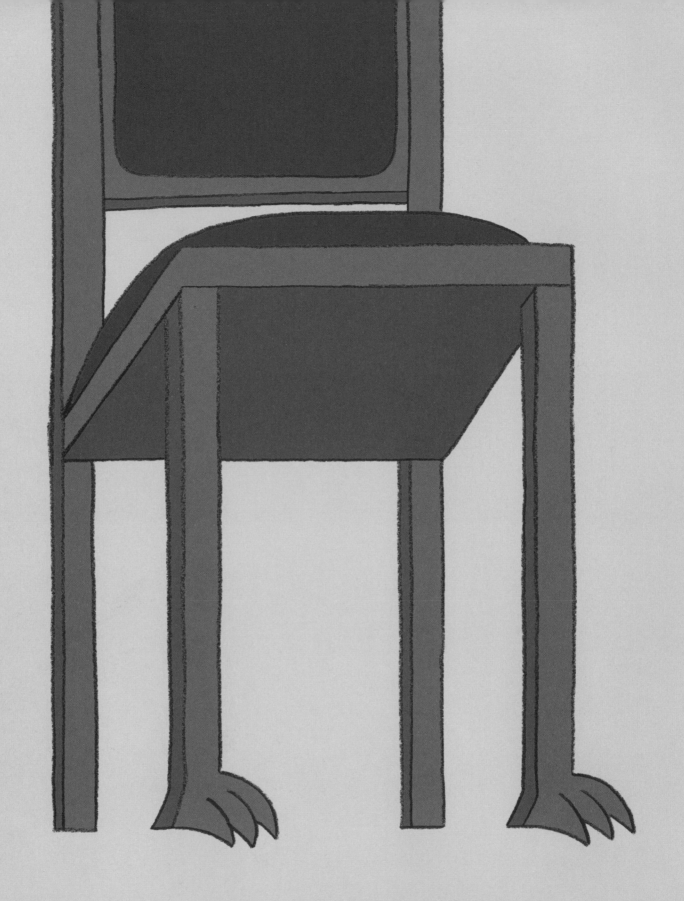

—WAS TOO TALL.
Goldilocks wasn't going to climb that high just to sit
in some chair, so she hiked over to the bedroom.

When she got there, Goldilocks noticed
that the beds were also gigantically big.
"What is going on around here!?" groaned
the exhausted girl. "The bears that
live here must be nuts!"

Just then the room filled with a loud, booming noise that was either a passing truck or a Dinosaur gloating, "A FEW MORE MINUTES AND SHE'LL BE ASLEEP! DELICIOUS CHOCOLATE-FILLED-LITTLE-GIRL-BONBONS ARE YUMMIER WHEN THEY'RE RESTED!"

Even a little girl who never listens to anyone or anything had to hear *that*.

HOME
SWEET
DINOSAU→
HOME

Goldilocks took a minute to stop and think, which was longer than she was used to stopping and thinking.

"Hey . . ." she told herself. "This isn't some bear's house. This is some DINOSAUR'S house!"

Say what you like about Goldilocks,
but she was no fool. As quickly as she could,
she ran to the back door and *got out of there!*

Just then a loud plane flew by, which sounded pretty much like a trio of Dinosaurs yelling "NOW!" or "CHARGE!" or the Norwegian expression for "CHEWY-BONBON-TIME!"

Suddenly—and completely coincidentally—the three Dinosaurs rushed through the front door.

But they were too late.

Goldilocks was gone, and all that was left in the house were three disappointed Dinosaurs.

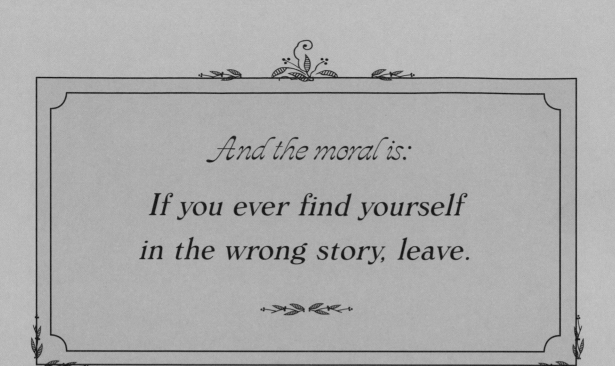

And the moral is:

If you ever find yourself
in the wrong story, leave.

And the moral for Dinosaurs is:

LOCK THE BACK DOOR!

Goldilocks and the Three Musketeers

Goldilocks and the Three Free Men

Goldilocks and the Three Xylophones

Goldilocks and the Three Poodles

Goldilocks and the Three Dudes

Goldilocks and the Three Red Herring

Goldilocks and the Three Wall Street Types

Goldilocks and the Three Crows

Goldilocks and the Three Owls

Goldilocks and the Three Bus Drivers

Goldilocks and the Three Termites

Goldilocks and the Three Hip

Goldilocks and the Three Worms

Goldilocks and the Three Drummers

Goldilocks and the Three Wise Men

Goldilocks and the Three Condors

Goldilocks and the Three Rats

Goldilocks and the Three Major M

Goldilocks and the Three Squid

Goldilocks and the Three Gerbils

Goldilocks and the Three Foot-Long Hoagies

Goldilocks and the Three Prairie Dogs

Goldilocks and the Three-Piece

Goldilocks and the Three Bedbugs

Goldilocks and the Three Frogs

Goldilocks and the Three Deer

Goldilocks and the Three Glasses

Dedicated to Lee and Diane, dinosaurs

Balzer + Bray is an imprint of HarperCollins Publishers.

Goldilocks and the Three Dinosaurs. Copyright © 2012 by Mo Willems.
a division of HarperCollins Publishers, 195 Broadway, New York, NY 10007.
www.harpercollinschildrens.com

Library of Congress Cataloging-in-Publication Data is available.
ISBN 978-0-06-210418-2

Typography by Martha Rago
15 16 17 SCP 10 9 8
❖
First Edition